THE VERY
ITCHY BEAR

NICK BLAND

Scholastic Canada Ltd.
Toronto New York London Auckland Sydney
Mexico City New Delhi Hong Kong Buenos Aires

For Walter.

Scholastic Canada Ltd.
604 King Street West, Toronto, Ontario M5V 1E1, Canada

Scholastic Inc.
557 Broadway, New York, NY 10012, USA

Scholastic Australia Pty Limited
PO Box 579, Gosford, NSW 2250, Australia

Scholastic New Zealand Limited
Private Bag 94407, Botany, Manukau 2163, New Zealand

Scholastic Children's Books
Euston House, 24 Eversholt Street, London NW1 1DB, UK

www.scholastic.ca

Library and Archives Canada Cataloguing in Publication

Bland, Nick, 1973-, author, illustrator
The very itchy bear / Nick Bland.

Previously published: 2011.
ISBN 978-1-4431-6311-8 (softcover)

I. Title.
PZ10.3.B527Ver 2018   j823'.92   C2017-904026-X

5 4 3 2 1   Printed in China 38   18 19 20 21 22

Bear is here . . .

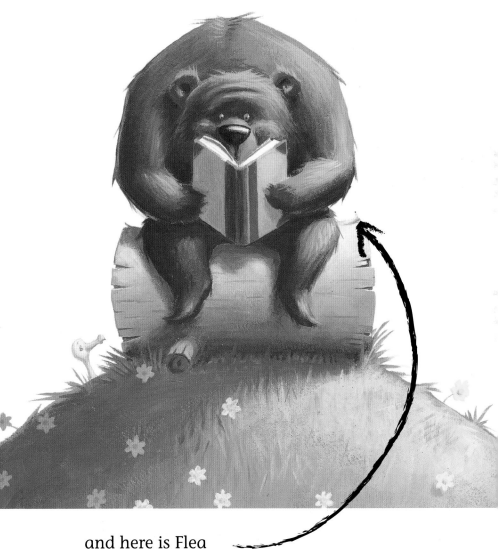

and here is Flea
(but Flea's a little small to see).

This is Flea about to bite,
but not because he's impolite.

He's biting Bear to say, "Hello!,"

biting high

and biting low.

This is Flea biting Bear
under here

and over there.

Biting, biting everywhere!

This is Bear and this is Flea,
floating, floating out to sea.

This is Bear not quite sure
if Flea is with him any more.

This is Flea reminding Bear . . .

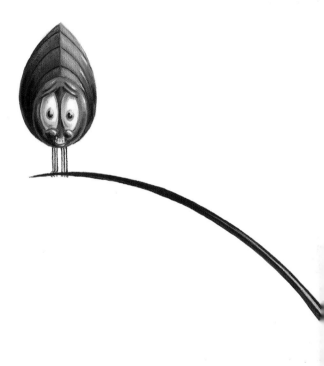

that Flea has not gone anywhere.

This is Bear flicking Flea

off his fur and out to sea.

This is Bear all alone,
frightened now he's on his own.

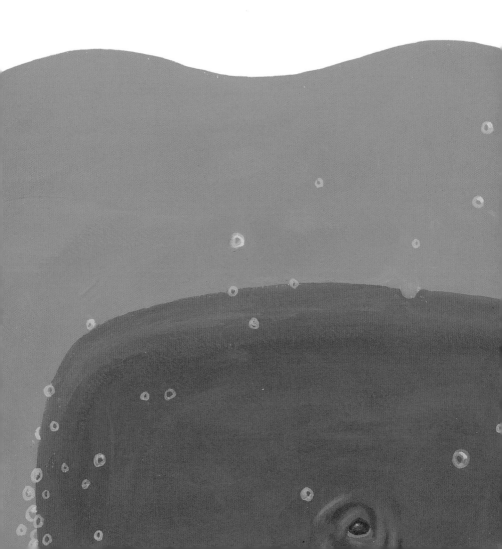

This is Bird
and this is Bear
and Flea is way, way over there.

This is Flea about to see
how scary hungry birds can be!

This is Bear in the sea
swimming fast to rescue Flea.

Flea is happy Bear can swim.
This is Flea not biting him.

This is Flea and this is Bear.
Together they go everywhere.